BLUE HANDED

BLUE HANDED

TWO BOYS. ONE THIEF.

WRITTEN BY MATHEA MAE

Printed with LuLu Press, Inc

Printed by LuLu Press, Inc., in the United States of America.

1. Portions of this book are works of fiction. Any references to historical events, real people, or real places are used fictitiously. Other names, characters, places and events are products of the author's imagination, and any resemblances to actual events or places or persons, living or dead, is entirely coincidental.

2. Portions of this book are works of nonfiction. Certain names and identifying characteristics have been changed.

ISBN: 978-1-79486-890-8

First printing, 2020.

LuLu Press, Inc
Morrisville, North Carolina USA
lulu.com

This book is dedicated to my Grandpa, Don Heidel.
I'll love you always.

PREFACE

This was one of the more challenging pieces that I have written, based on a true story about my Grandpa, but with not much information to go off of it was my job to fictitiously take the reins.

Taking a piece of reality and molding it into my own story, although challenging, was incredibly fun and an overall growing experience. I am just so thankful to have gotten the chance to tell his story, and put my own words to it.

This story takes place in the late 1950s to early 1960s in a high school in Pewaukee, Wisconsin, surrounding a series of thefts and how they reached their unexpected conclusion.

THE AUTHOR

MATHEA MAE, 2020

ACKNOWLEDGMENTS

Thank you to everyone that helped making this story a reality, and a very special thanks to my mom for pushing me to actually get this done, and for my Grandpa for being the living and breathing inspiration.

BLUE HANDED

Donny, age 16, September '59, he had to write over and over again. Filling out workbooks was boring. Why did he need good penmanship anyway? It's not like he was going to ever do anything around here. Nothing interesting ever happens. But, at least next was one of his favorite classes-gym.

He slipped off his shoes to change into his gym shorts, hanging his jeans on the rack alongside the other boys'.

"You ready for the one on one today?" Donny asked Sid with a smile.

The two friends walked into their gym class.

"You better believe it!" Their conversation was cut short by a one *Richie Mayes,* slamming his fist into the wall.

"This is *not* funny!" he shouted. "Who took my money?"

His question was answered in a silence not often found in a group of high-schoolers. Donny and Sid shared a glance, no one wanted to be at the receiving end Richie's anger.

Donny observed as Richie pushed his way towards Ron, the token 'math wizard' with a frail frame.

"Did you take my money?" he sneered down at the smaller boy.

Ron trembled in fear as Richie grabbed him by his collar.

"Hey, leave him alone," Donny said taking a step towards the two boys, intending to stop the fight before it really started.

"Why? D'you take my money? I had 3 dollars in there! I was saving for months!" Richie said now directing his anger to Donny.

"Boys, please. What seems to be the problem?" Mr. Colburn, the gym teacher, asked stepping into the room.

William spoke up first. Although only recently transferring, he took no time in establishing his presence in the school. "Richie was just upset because he lost his money. He probably just left it at home, along with his manners."

This earned him a stern glare from Richie, and snickers from the rest of the students. Not missing a beat Mr. Colburn directed all attention back to him.

"I'd like to remind you all whose time we're on? Let's get to work!"

***

"Do you think Richie really had his money stolen?" Sid asked Donny as they sat for lunch.

"I don't doubt it. Francis didn't want a ton of folks to know this, but," Donny leaned in closer to Sid,

"He lost his money last week, too." Donny nodded at Sid's disbelief.

"Said it was in his pant pockets, then after he changed back into them after gym, he couldn't find it anywhere. Said he looked all over the school, must've been taken."

"So somebody's runnin' 'round taking our money? Did he tell a teacher or somethin'?" Sid asked.

"You know Francis, he's no fink. Everyone knows his Dad his still 'in-between jobs', who'd steal from him, knowing that?"

Sid shook his head "S'not right."

"No. It's not right,"

***

It was two weeks later before another incident of stolen money, but since no one owned up to the crime, and the boys couldn't prove they didn't just lose it, authorities did nothing. Teachers warned students not to bring money to the school, but besides that, there was nothing they could do.

"This is why you gotta bring 'ur own lunch," Sid said flapping his homemade sandwich in the air for emphasis.

"Then I don't gotta deal with money at school at all. All the pickpocket will get from me is lint!"

Donny laughed with his friend, but his mind was on something else. His gaze falling on William Ledford sitting across the room. He sat tall and smug, but there was something else there... He caught Donny's gaze and winked at him.

"There's something off about him."

"Who?" Sid asked, still face deep in his lunch.

"William. He's been here, what, a month? Isn't that when the first wallet was emptied?"

"You may be onto somthin' here. He doesn't seem like a guy that would be opposed to the five finger discount. But, why'd he go to the trouble of robin' us? Look at him, he never had to pay for a thing in his life."

Sid was right, William was always donned with an on-brand button-up shirt, neatly pressed, tucked into his slacks. Even when he changed for gym it was always the highest that money could buy. Donny often wondered why William's parents hadn't transferred him to a nicer school.

"Maybe he's just lookin' for somthin fun to do, I dunno." Sid offered.

***

Weeks continued like this, accusations were flying between students, authorities is the school did nothing, and more kids lost money. Donny figured that this was the new normal now, threats of stolen money and people fretting over if someone will steal their possessions until they all graduated.

The huffing of Principal Baines interrupted Donny's thoughts. He entered the school cafeteria with a scowl on his face, still red from rushing. Why he was in such a hurry Donny had no clue. Then Donny realized maybe the redness of Principal Baine's face was more from anger than anything else.

He planted himself in the middle of the crowd looking extremely displeased. Clearing his throat he moved himself to a higher position. "I would like to ask the person who is responsible for stealing the money from the other students to please fess up. Now." he looked across the room, having gotten everyone's attention by now. "If you admit to it now, your punishment will be much less severe."

Students murmured and some whispered laughter seemed to come from everywhere and nowhere, but no one spoke up. Donny stole a glance at William, he was smirking at the Principal, and mocking him under his breath.

Turning to Sid Donny whispered, "I really think it's William, or he at least knows something."

"Or he's just being a teenage brat? But, yeah, maybe it's 'im. Gotta be somebody." Then Sid's face contorted into more theatrical expression. "Or! It isn't somebody! It's....some*thing*. Think about it, an *alien* opening up portals to grab our money?! Definitely what's happenin'."

"Where'd you get portals from, pal?"

"Well, the government wants you to think that aliens use spaceships, right? But they actually use portals, because, how else would they get to earth? Unless they have a lot better gas mileage than us!" The two boys burst out laughing before they realized that Principal Baines was still nearby. Luckily he didn't seem to notice them out of the crowd, but Donny spotted Coach Colburn shaking his head disappointingly at them from the other side of the room.

"I promise you, I will find whoever did this. And there *will* be serious consequences." With that, the Principal strode out of the room.

"Wonder what made him care all of the sudden?" Sid thought.

"Yeah. I wonder."

Math class was long. Donny was good at it, but right now he wished he was doing anything else at the moment. A knock on the door halted the class, the two teachers whispered between the doorway. Donny's math teacher turned back to the mostly bored class. "Donald White, and Sidney Campbell. Please report to the Principal's office."

It turns out there *was* something that he wouldn't rather be doing.

Donny and Sid got up to follow the teacher out the door, trying to avoid the snickering and occasional sympathetic look from fellow students.

You'd think they would call us when he was ready to meet, Donny thought to himself as the two boys sat shrunken on the bench awaiting the Principal. Sid was as silent as Donny has ever heard him, he was terrified too, no doubt.

By the time they actually met with the Principal, both boys had run through all the worst-case scenarios on how this could turn out.

"Do you know why I called you in here today?"

They shook their heads. "No, sir."

The full little man huffed with authority. He did that a lot. Donny couldn't tell if it was a breathing problem or if it just made him feel superior to respond without having to form words.

"You two are here today because," he glanced between them, pausing longer than necessary. Or maybe it just felt longer.

"*I* know you didn't do it. To be quite frank with you, you two are the *only* ones I know who didn't do it. Steal I mean, if you didn't catch on."

Donny could breathe again, he shared a relieved look with Sid before refocusing on the Principal.

"It has come to my attention that this school has become a hot pocket for crime." he leaned back in his chair. "specifically, your grade." Another too-long pause.

"You two are good kids. You stick up for each other as well as others. You've shown respect, and truth be told, I just trust you."

"Uh, thank you." Donny stammered.

Sid looked surprised, but the compliments didn't do much but boost his ego. "All due respect, sir, but why are you suddenly taking an interest? It's been months since it started,"

The Principal looked down, his ears turned a darker shade of red. "If you must know, my son, Tom, was robbed yesterday."

Donny knew Tom, he was quarterback, as football captain Donny had a lot of practices with him.

"That tracks," Sid shrugged, done with interrogating.

"So, sir, why did you call us in here? We don't know who did it." Donny brought up.

"Ah. Yes. You see, my brother… well he's a character. Anyway. He is obsessed with all this stuff," the Principal gestured at nothing in particular. "'True Crime' and all that nonsense. Last night, I may have brought it up about the happenings of the school. He said he might be able to help."

"Like, solve the crime?"

"Yes. No- well, I'll just let him explain it." With that the Principal nodded and stood up, leaving the boys by themselves still trying to process.

Couldn't get any weirder than that, Donny thought. He was wrong.

Enter: Charles Baines. Crime fanatic. He was tall and lanky, quite the opposite of his brother. His demeanor the opposite too, while Principal Baines gave off a very standoffish and unapproachable vibe, Charles seemed...trustworthy. Friendly. *This must be what they mean when they say someone is charismatic*, Donny guessed.

"Nice to meet you, boys. I hear we're going to catch a culprit together?"

They shrugged.

He didn't push them to talk, just took a seat loosely in the principal's chair and leaned in closer to them, his elbows sprawling over the desk.

"Any suspects? Unsavory characters? Suspicious actions? Or maybe somebody that's just barely there, seemingly melting into the background?" Charles said with such energy but somehow didn't come off as unhinged.

"Well, there is this one kid... William Ledford. He transferred here a while back, and we think he might be hiding something."

"Well, we're going to catch whoever it is blue handed."

"Blue handed?"

"Yeah, issnit red-handed?" Sid asked.

Nicholas's eyes shone as his whole face crinkled into a smile, "It would be...if I bought the red option." he rummaged through his satchel and took out a jar full of white powder. "We sprinkle some of this in your wallets, and when the thief touches it, it will stick," Charles said as if it was the best thing he had ever heard. "The best part is when it gets wet, it turns blue."

Donny blinked.

"So, when he takes our money, we'll be able to see it later?"

"Exactly! It doesn't wash off easily. He'll never see it coming!"

"How are *we* going to help?" Donny asked, glancing at the clock. This may be interesting but they were going to be late for 4th period.

Charles seemed to sense his urgency and began to wrap up."Tomorrow pour this into your wallets. Make sure that they are accessible, and tell as *many* people as you can, organically, that you're going out after. Insinuate that you're carrying a lot of cash, and then, we wait."

Sid was the first boy to break the silence. "Wow. You really *are* good at this."

***

"Yeah, I'mma get a brand new spankin' bike. Brought enough bread to buy the nicest one they got." Sid told Sally.

Donny shook his head, no *way* was Sally Rimmer the one taking their money, but Sid would take any excuse he could to talk to the blonde.

William overheard, "Finally aged out of your training wheels Campbell?"

Sid glared at him before turning his back. If he lost it now, he might say something that would spoil days of setup. Donny and Sid expected their money to get stolen the first day, but for some reason, their plan was still yet to be set in motion.

"Okay kids, back to class," said Ms. Hubert, herding the restless kids out of the hall.

William led the way to the locker room, his stride the same as usual, overcompensating. Changing into shorts and William to his spare shoes, the boys made their way out to wait for Coach Colburn, he was always late, but still expected the class to be on time. It had been at least 5 minutes of just standing around goofing off.

"Hey, I forgot my water bottle, be right back," Sid said before sprinting back towards the locker room.

Donny didn't think twice about it before his friend returned, no water bottle, but an expression that might be described as a cross between excitement and disbelief.

"Donny! Our money! It's gone!"

Donny's mouth dropped. "Really?" his head swung back from Sid to the other students, including William. "But-everyone is in here. Who would have time to-" Donny's voice cut off at the sight of Coach Colburn walking in.

All eyes were on him.

"Hey uh, Coach," Richie said, hesitantly. "You got something on your..." he gestured vaguely.

Coach Colburn looked down at himself, seeing his hands stained blue, and growing bluer by the second.

"You?" Donny gaped.

"What? I-" he tried frantically to wipe off the blue on his shirt, nothing helped. "There must be-there must be something in the faucet. Or is this a...a... senior prank?" he stammered

Sid and Donny caught eyes and wordlessly exchanged a message before Sid broke off running again, this time to get the Principal.

"The faucet," Donny said slowly to make sure he had his attention. "You washed your hands recently?"

"Well, yeah, just before I got in here, do you know something about this Donald?"

Donny smiled, "You could say that. What were you doing before you washed your hands?"

"I mean- I was in the bathroom and I.." Coach's embarrassment turned him red. "I'll have you written up for this!"

"I doubt it. In fact, I think the Principal would like to learn about some of the activities you do here. Instead of teaching us."

"What are you on about?" William asked, trying to keep up.

"He's the one that has been stealing our money."

Chaos erupted from the class, angry voices rose and friends had to stop others from rushing their coach.

"Silence." Principal Baines commanded entering the gymnasium. "Phil. I heard you got something...on your hands?"

Coach Colburn knitted his brow, he couldn't keep up with what was happening "I-these kids-I just...."

Principal Baines huffed in disappointment. "I thought you were better than this."

"What's happening? How did you know he did it?" William asked, gaining in frustration.

"The blue on his hands," Donny started. "that was on mine and Sid's wallets. Now our money is gone, and his hands are blue."

This was enough to convince the class, and the authorities as well. Colburn realized he had dug himself too deep, he didn't even put up a fight. With a quick search of Philip's possessions turned up a lot of unaccountable cash, undoubtedly stolen.

After Phil Colburn was fired, things went back to normal. Well, as normal as a high school can be. Turns out all William was hiding was the fact that he was failing classes and needed a tutor. I guess not everything is as thrilling as catching a thief. And maybe everyone was not as perfect as they seemed. Donny pondered as he and Sid walked side by side on their way home from school.

Gym was actually fun now, with their new coach. Francis's dad stepped in, he was still looking for a job and the school a new teacher.

"So, just because it wasn't aliens doesn't mean it *couldn't* have been!"

"With their...portals?"

"Yes! With the portals! We gotta watch out Donny."

"You know, I think we'll be alright." Donny sighed with content. This is how it should be.

"Hey, y'know what I just thought of?" asked Sid.

"Hmm?"

"There actually *was* something interesting that happened in this town for once!"

AFTERWORD

I had heard the basis for this story many times through my Mom and she through my Grandpa, and it was her who actually pushed me into immortalizing it as this book.

When my Grandpa was in high school he really *was* recruited to be bait to help catch a thief along side another boy, who's name was forgotten along with many other details, but we really do know that it was a teacher that was eventually caught with blue on his hands.

Although this is based off real events, all characters in this story are fictitious, there was no Charles Baines or William Ledford, I had to create a world around the details that we knew.

(Donny at age 17)

DON HEIDEL

Don Heidel is the real life 'Donny'. In 1943 he was born in the cold of February in a taxi cab on the way to the hospital in downtown Milwaukee.

He didn't grow up with money, but that didn't stop him from always trying to help people.

He became a social worker at around the age of 25, but he was always still looking for ways to make the world a better place, so in 1973 he, along with two friends, started Chileda Institute.

Chileda is an organization that gives care and treatment for children and young adults with developmental disabilities.

He has done so much more for this world then most, and I am so incredibly proud to call him my grandfather.

(Don at age 74)